MORTON COUNTY LIBRARY
10065

W9-BVK-258

The Berenstain Bears' REPORT CARD TROUBLE

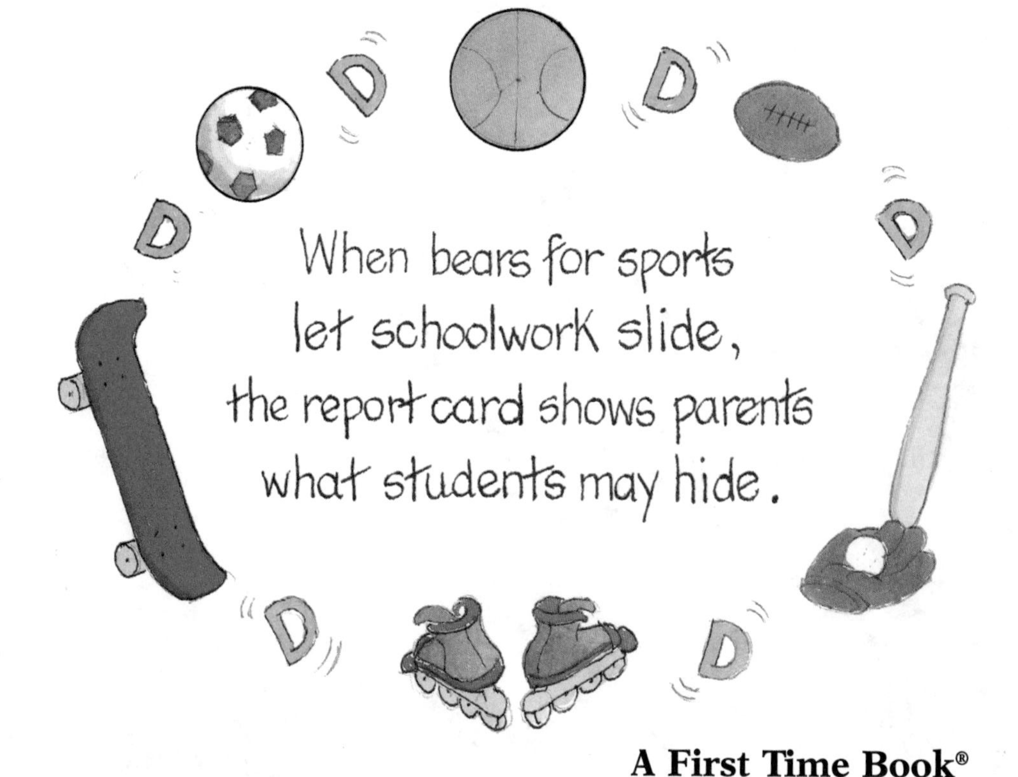

When bears for sports
let schoolwork slide,
the report card shows parents
what students may hide.

A First Time Book®

The Berenstain Bears' REPORT CARD TROUBLE

Stan & Jan Berenstain

Random House New York

Published in the United States by Random House, Inc., New York, and simultaneously in Canada by Random House of Canada Limited, Toronto.
www.randomhouse.com/kids www.berenstainbears.com
Library of Congress Cataloging-in-Publication Data
Berenstain, Stan. The Berenstain Bears' report card trouble / by Stan & Jan Berenstain.
p. cm. – (A first time book) SUMMARY: When Brother Bear spends too much time on sports and brings home a terrible report card, the whole family pitches in to help him improve his grades.
ISBN 0-375-81127-3 (trade) — ISBN 0-375-91127-8 (lib. bdg.)
[1. Homework—Fiction. 2. Sports—Fiction. 3. Family life—Fiction. 4. Bears—Fiction.]
I. Title: Report card trouble. II. Berenstain, Jan. III. Title.
PZ7.B4483 Bfeg 2002 [Fic]—dc21 2001048316
Printed in the United States of America First Edition May 2002 10 9 8 7 6 5 4 3 2 1

It was report card day at Bear Country School.

And there they were in their envelopes on each desk when Brother's class returned from lunch.

Most of Brother's classmates sat right down, took their report cards out of their envelopes, and looked at them.

But not Brother. He just sat there and stared at the envelope.

Most of Brother's classmates were pleased with their marks. Most of them had gotten A's, B's, and a few C's.

But Brother stared at the envelope as if it were a bomb about to go off.

He picked it up and ever so slowly drew the report card out of the envelope.

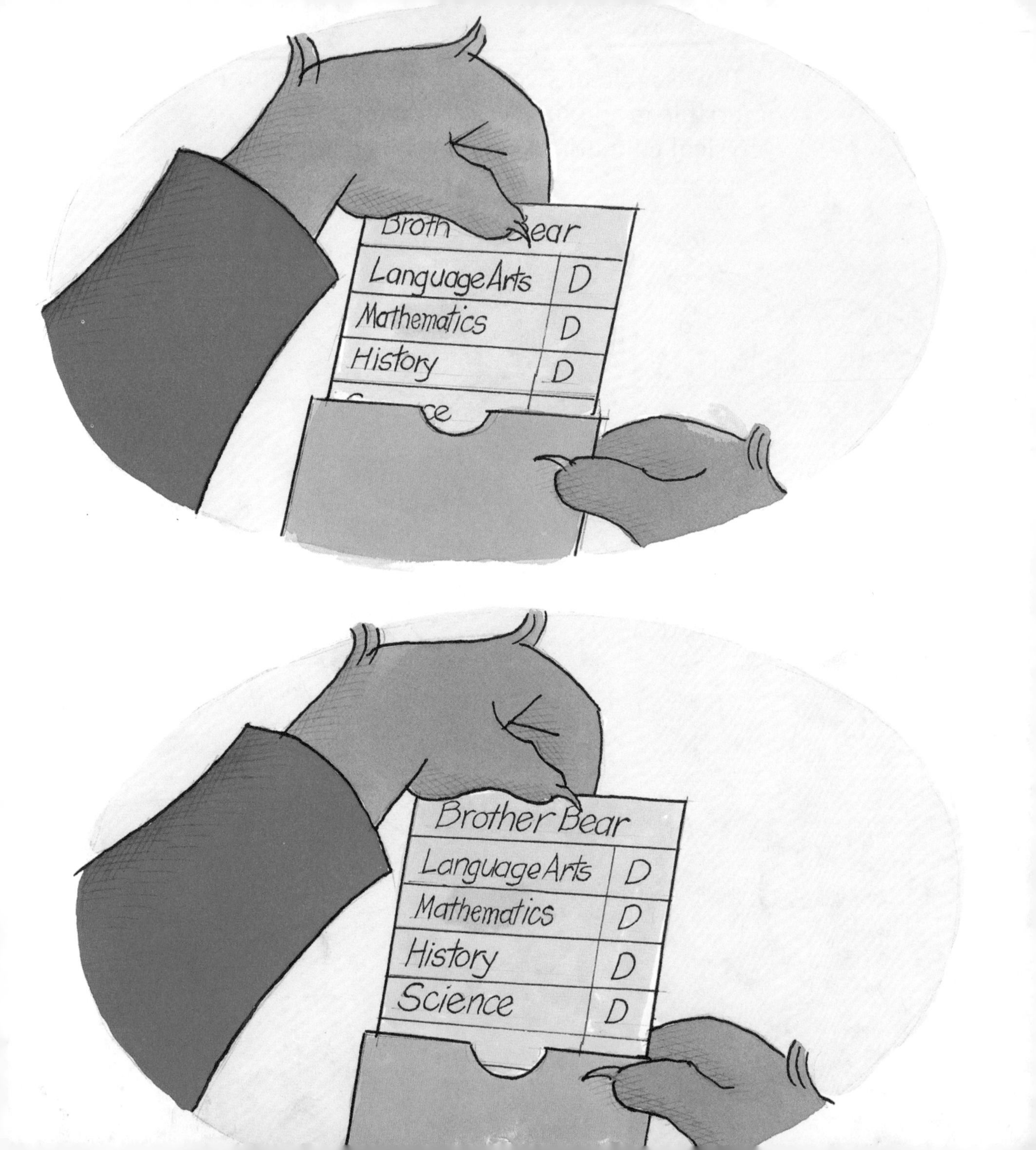
Language Arts D
Mathematics D
History D
Brother Bear
Language Arts D
Mathematics D
History D
Science D

It was a clean sweep. Brother had gotten a terrible grade in every subject except . . . physical education!

If Teacher Bob had given out A-pluses in physical education, Brother would have gotten one. That was because in addition to being captain and star goalie on the soccer team, Brother ran track, pitched baseball, and did gymnastics like a monkey.

That was the problem.

Brother was so taken up with sports that he had let his other subjects slide, slide, slide. It hadn't happened overnight and perhaps Mama and Papa should have seen it coming. But what with one thing and another, they hadn't.

And now Brother was in the soup, deep in the soup up to his eyeballs.

Sister was waiting at the bus when school let out. She had gotten a great report card and wanted to tell Brother about it. "Brother! Brother! Guess what?" she cried. "I got three A's and two B's! The best report card I ever . . ." But she didn't finish.

She could tell from Brother's face that he must have gotten a very bad report card. He was looking straight ahead and walking like a robot. They climbed onto the bus.

"Who's your zombie friend?" asked Lizzy Bruin, Sister's best friend.

Sister mouthed, "Got . . . a . . . bad . . . report card." Sister sat with Lizzy. Brother sat across the aisle. He stared straight ahead as the bus drove away from the school.

Later, Mama and Sister watched from the
ext room as Papa looked at Brother's report
ard. Sister put her fingers in her ears to
nuffle the explosion. But Papa didn't
xplode—not at first.

Then came the biggest explosion ever
eard in the tree house.

It shook the earth.

It trembled the trees.

It scared small animals into their
idey-holes.

Papa said all the things papas say when they see a really bad report card.

THIS IS THE WORST REPORT I HAVE EVER SEEN!
IT'S A DISGRACE, AN OUTRAGE!
TO THINK THAT ANY SON OF MINE...
Brother Bear
Language Arts D
Mathematics D
History D
Science D
Physical Ed. A
Sig.:

"Well," said Papa, staring down at Brother, "what have you got to say for yourself?"

"I guess I'm grounded," said Brother.

"That's right!" roared Papa. "Grounded! Grounded, grounded, grounded! There'll be no more TV, no more video games, no more movies, no more skateboarding, no more rollerblading, no more soccer, no more sports of any kind. And furthermore—"

When Mama saw a tear forming in Brother's eye and his lip beginning to tremble, she came to his rescue.

"That will be quite enough shouting," she said. "But your father's right, Brother. You're going to be grounded until you pull your marks up."

"But that'll take forever," said Brother. "It's like being grounded for life."

"Be that as it may, that's the way it's going to be!" said Papa.

Mama watched as Brother slowly climbed the stairs and went into his room. She knew he would find in his room all the things he wasn't going to be allowed to do until he pulled his marks up: his skateboard, his rollerblades, his soccer ball, his baseball and glove, his video games, and his walls covered with pictures of sports heroes.

He didn't stay in his room long. He came back down again. Mama wasn't surprised. She could almost see a cloud of gloom over his head as he wandered from one room to another, a lost soul in his own house.

Papa started to turn the TV on, but Mama caught his eye and shook her head *no*. Brother noticed.

He went outside and sat on the front steps. Mama came out and sat on the steps with him. Papa and Sister watched from the inside.

"You know, it's not the end of the world, dear," said Mama.

"It may as well be," said Brother.

"All you have to do is pull your marks up," said Mama.

"By the time I pull my marks up, ›ccer season will be over. Since I ın't do anything else, I guess I etter start hitting the books."

:e went back into ıe house.

Supper that night was pretty glum. It was as if the whole house were grounded. Mama and Sister cleared the table quickly so Brother could use it to work on his studies.

"Hey, look," said Papa as he scanned the paper, "there's a pretty good movie playing at the multiplex. What do you say we take in a . . ."

But Papa didn't finis[h] because Mama frowne[d] and shook her head *no*. There was no way the rest of the family was going to take in a movi[e] while Brother was hom[e] struggling with fraction[s] and percentages.

Word that Brother was grounded got around quickly the next day. Coach Grizzmeyer was pretty disappointed when he heard about it. The team had some big soccer matches coming up and they wouldn't have much of a chance without their star goalie.

After school, Sister came into the kitchen with a long face and slumped on a chair.

"What are you moping about? You're not grounded," said Mama.

"No," said Sister, "but I may as well be. With Brother grounded, I've got nobody to do stuff with—play video games, rollerblade, practice soccer, or anything."

"You could go over to Lizzy's," suggested Mama. "She's your best friend."

"Maybe so," said Sister. "But she's not much of a rollerblader, her mother doesn't allow her to play video games, and as for soccer—forget it."

That evening, Mama took Papa aside. “My dear,” she said, “I’m just as disappointed in Brother’s report card as you are, but in a way we’re almost as much to blame as Brother.”

“We *are*?” said Papa.

“That’s right,” said Mama. “There’s more to being a parent than cheering at soccer games. We should have been checking on his work.”

“What do you think we should do?” asked Papa.

“I think he’s having a hard time with fractions and percentages. You used to be a whiz at that sort of thing. Why don’t you help him?”

But it turned out that
Papa was pretty rusty, so
Mama helped *both* of them.

Even Sister pitched in. She quizzed Brother on his new vocabulary words.

The family lost track of time and got to bed late.

It was more of the same the next evening. But besides his regular homework, Brother had to make a model of the solar system. Luckily, Mama had enough fruits and vegetables on hand to do the job.

And just as they had the night before, the whole family pitched in.

By the time Brother got home from school the next day, Papa had had enough. (It helped that Brother had gotten a B in a fractions-and-percentages quiz and an A for his solar system.) “Look,” said Papa, “everybody wants me to ease up on you—your sister, your friends . . . I even had a call from your soccer coach. And I’m willing. But you’ve got to promise that you’ll pull your grades up and that you’ll never fall behind again.”

"I promise," said Brother. "I don't want to get a report card like that *ever again*."

"Good!" said Papa. "That's a big load off my mind. Because I don't ever want to go through being grounded again."

"Me neither," said Sister.

"Me neither," said Mama.

"Me neither," said Brother with a big gri